The
Rare
One

Also by Pamela Rogers

The Weekend

THE
RARE
ONE

by
Pamela Rogers

THOMAS NELSON INC.
NASHVILLE / NEW YORK

Copyright © 1973, 1974 by Pamela Rogers

All rights reserved under International and Pan-American Conventions. Published by Thomas Nelson Inc., Nashville, Tennessee. Manufactured in the United States of America.

First U.S. edition

Library of Congress Cataloging in Publication Data

Rogers, Pamela.
  The rare one.

  SUMMARY: Unhappy about his father's remarriage, thirteen-year-old Toby finds friendship with an old man living alone in the woods.
  [1. Friendship—Fiction] I. Title.
PZ7. R6365Rar3   [Fic]   74–10286
ISBN 0–8407–6414–6

The
Rare
One

Chapter One

Three of the four walls were in darkness. Across the fourth raced the golden spotted form of a leopard.

The film whirred on, to the accompaniment of the narrator's final buildup.

"And so we must leave them—in the hope that by our actions now, we can preserve them for our children and our children's children—"

Toby shifted in his seat. While the film had been on, he had been enthralled—but the flowery windup had broken the spell. It was like politicians, always spouting on about Freedom and God and Mankind.

"Pull up the shades, please," said Miss Hardcastle.

The eighth grade stretched themselves. The sunlight, bursting in, screwed up their eyes, and released their tongues.

All except Toby's. The film, while it lasted, had proved a satisfactory sort of escape. Now reality was breaking in on all sides. Already chairs were being stacked at the back of the hall. It was nearly time for the bell. It rang shrilly.

Like a leaf caught in the eddy, Toby went downstream to the cloakroom. The outside door opening let in the icy blasts of air, frost-crisped in spite of the sun. The warm safety of being one of a crowd began to break up. The atoms were separating—each returning to a different home.

"Coming, Toby?" called a friend, David, pausing at the door. "Or are you waiting?"

"Coming. Coming," called Toby feverishly, suddenly galvanized into action—his cap thrust over his thatch of hair, his duffel coat dragged on.

"Great film," he said. Anything to keep talking, to seem preoccupied, as he went out. She was there. She had waited. He could see her green coat and fur hat out of the corner of his eye. Ma.

"Hey . . . there's Mrs. . . . er . . . your 'mother' "

"Come on," said Toby. "I've got to get back early."

Out of the corner of his eye, he could see the green arm, half raised in greeting, fall.

"Good," he thought.

"Hey, hang on," said David, half running after him.

Toby felt his eyes turned on him, half curious, half amused. He set his head down, as if in the grip of a gale, and forged on.

"There was a time when you liked her," said David, with a bland sort of innocence. "Now that she's married to your dad, you can't stand her. What's she done, for heaven's sake?"

The red rose up in Toby's fair skin. He set his mouth tight.

"Well?"

"Shut up. Shut up!"

David stopped. "Suit yourself," he said. "I'm not walking home with you in this foul mood."

"Go on then. Go on," said Toby.

David merged with another group. Toby walked the last street alone.

"A loner," he thought. "I'm a loner." The phrase sounded good. He held up his head higher. His eyes looked up. He swaggered a little.

"Hello."

Toby stopped dead in his tracks.

"To-o-by."

Toby glanced backward quickly—thin as a wire, with her tow hair glinting white, Olly pursued him.

She smiled happily at him through her pink-rimmed glasses.

"Teeth like tombstones," thought Toby.

"Wasn't it lucky catching you," she said, swinging her case of books.

"Crammed full, of course—little grind," thought Toby.

"We were late today. Gosh, I'm starving, aren't you?"

9

Toby tried to look through her. If his father *had* to marry again, why did it have to be with an attachment like Olly for a stepsister?

"Are you all right?" said Olly. "Your eyes have a long-range sort of look."

Toby's eyes swiveled back into focus.

"Go away," he said.

Olly looked at him.

"You're not feeling sociable?" she said.

"No," said Toby.

Olly nodded. "Well, I believe in respecting other people's feelings," she said. "I'll keep quiet."

Toby walked along, surrounded by the silence. Ten years old she was—three years younger than he—and far too clever.

He kicked the gate open. The back-door key was under the ledge. It stuck in the lock, as it always did. He struggled with it.

"Am I to be invisible as well as silent?" said Olly.

Toby handed her the key. She opened the door.

"It's a knack," she said apologetically, dipping her glasses in a quick bob of her head.

A delicious smell wafted out to meet them. There was a time when he used to come home to an empty house—no food cooked, no fire laid.

The house had been *his*. *He* would light the fire. *He* would set the table and when his father came in *he* would cook their meal.

Olly opened the oven door and sniffed reverently.

"Praise the Lord for automatic ovens and beef casserole," she said.

Toby's insides did a traitorous rumble. He went to the pantry and cut a slice of bread.

"You'll spoil your appetite," said Olly. "You know they won't be long."

"Mind your own business," said Toby.

"There's apple pie and ice cream," said Olly.

Toby picked up even more bread than he had intended.

"I'm going to my room," he said. "I'm going to do my homework. And I don't want your company, thank you."

"I'm going to my room to work on *my* project," said Olly with dignity. "So I won't *need* your company."

In Toby's room everything was the same as it had always been. He defended it jealously from new paint or wallpaper. He walked over to the window and stared out.

That was the same too. The garden sloped steeply down—you could see quite a way, over the next road, to the beginning of the woods. Everything else was brown and gray, but the woods were still green. So many of its trees were evergreen, creeper, holly, laurel, rhododendron, gradually winning over the oaks and the beech.

Toby sat down at his desk and flipped open his

11

books. "Poor—can do better," it said in red crabby letters under the smudged map of Africa. Toby turned back to earlier work, where the neat notes and colored diagrams blazoned remarks like "Good" and "Excellent work." He twisted his mouth in a smile—a sardonic smile, thought Toby, like the smile of that TV announcer. What *was* a sardonic smile, for heaven's sake? He got up and went to the mirror. Smile. Off. Sure—that was a sardonic one if ever there was one.

He'd do another ghastly piece of work. He didn't have to—but he would. His last report had shaken them up. Especially her . . . Ma.

This time last year it was flu time, and he had felt awful. Temperature, headache—everything. That's when it all had started, the visits from the school, first Mr. Cox, then Mrs. Sands. Her. Ma.

In this very room, he had sat up in bed and received them, along with the magazines and news from school. Feeling like a king—Toby made sounds of derision at himself, remembering—having them interested.

It was Mr. Cox, his homeroom teacher, who had stayed by his bed, playing card games, joking. The other—her—Mrs. Sands, had gone around the house with his father, praising the way they managed. His dad had blossomed out, shown off his collection of chrysanthemums. . . .

Back to school, he found a kind of glory in having been so ill—

"What's *she* like then?" they said.

Mrs. Sands was one of the senior staff. She taught the tenth grade only. The lower grades held her in a sort of horrified awe.

She was large and solid as a rock. She had dark eyes, which rested on you considering, summing you up. When she smiled, if she was pleased, the wrinkles radiated in stars and fans over her face like the sun breaking through a cloud.

Toby could get that smile. He felt a sort of reflected glory when her glance passed unknowing over his friends and came to him.

"Likes your dad, does she?" said one of the older girls.

Toby remembered coldly how fiercely he had denied it. She had visited *him*, hadn't she? As for his father needing anyone else—for nine years Toby and he had managed. They were a unit—together. They didn't need anybody.

But he was wrong. His father didn't find Toby enough. He had married Mrs. Sands quietly at the end of last term.

Wouldn't she have to be a widow, thought Toby, and why for heaven's sake did she have to have something like Olly to make things worse?

Toby stared at the wall behind which Olly was presumably working. Who would have thought that she, her, Ma—Toby made it sound like something not quite nice—could have produced skinny, pale Olly? Clever, brilliant Olly. Disconcerting Olly—who took insults, considered them, and then tried to discuss them. At ten years old. It was downright disgusting.

The sound of the door opening downstairs produced an answering scuttle of feet from the room next door.

Toby heard his father's voice too. They had come in together. Indiscriminately Olly was greeting them as if she hadn't seen them for years. Toby knew what she was doing—like a bur clinging to their arms—tongue going like mad—face beaming.

How his father lapped it up. Blossomed under it. Already he was beginning to lose that distinguished, fragile professor look. He looked settled, middle-aged, contented. . . .

"Toby. Toby. Toby." The voices called in turn.

Then he heard footsteps—hers—surprisingly light. She knocked on his door—oh, she was careful—and opened it.

"Food," she smiled. "Coming?"

Toby did a studied shrug, rather lost on her, as she was going down again. He followed slowly.

"The old order changeth, yielding place to new," Toby quoted to himself as he went down. By the time the bottom stair had been reached he was armored with that picture of himself—a lone knight pacing the shore, loyal to old ways and customs.

"Pass the salt. I said—pass the salt."

Toby, maintaining his faraway look, passed the salt to Olly.

"Some more?" said Ma.

Pride and stomach had a brief struggle. Toby passed his plate, not looking, as if he were passing along the offertory plate at church. He glanced up as the plate was taken. His father and Ma were exchanging glances; amusement glittered in them.

The warmth of their smile rested on him and Toby began to feel an answering expansion.

"Good day?" said his father.

"All right," said Toby. "There was this film about animals in danger of extinction."

Toby's father taught Biology at the local college. Studies of animals and their behavior were something of absorbing interest both to him and Toby.

"Seems to me," said Olly, "we ought to finish our stew before we start talking of animal preservation. I can control my veg-etarian" (she pronounced the word carefully) "instincts better *after* a good meal."

"Like Solomon in judgment," thought Toby resentfully. "Her with her long words." But his father and Ma were looking at her now.

"Then hurry up, and let's hear about Toby's film."

Olly gave a final swallow and smiled meekly at her mother. "Gone," she said.

"Not worth talking about," mumbled Toby, and retreated again to his self-made island.

Chapter Two

"You got an essay?"

Olly stood in the doorway of Toby's room, one sandal rubbing up and down her leg.

Toby kept his head down over his desk.

"I didn't hear you knock," he said.

"Oh."

Olly nodded and went out again. She knocked. After a minute's silence she poked her head around.

"Didn't you hear?" she said.

Toby flung his pencil down and turned around.

"For heaven's sake," he said. "Isn't anything private anymore? You're everywhere."

"You're obs-essed with privacy," said Olly. "I *like* company. What I said was have you got an essay—"

"Yes. Yes. I got an essay, and math and a map. Now I've got you. *That* is all I need."

Olly's eyes became hopeful.

"Can I help with the math?"

"Sure—oh yes—you can do it all. You're bound to be able to do it all—at ten years old."

Toby stopped short. He remembered that the first thing he had heard about Olly was that she was a mathematical whiz kid. From her father, they said. Just about all he had left.

Toby covered up his desperate notes too slowly. Olly was there, lips parted over the too-big teeth, white-blond hair falling on either side of her intent face.

She smiled beatifically. "Them," she said. "I know those." With a passionate absorption she wrote out the numbers.

Toby watched her, rage growing in him. What right had she to break into his room, do his homework, intrude? All the small routines set up by him and his father were being broken. The carefully knit circle enclosing them was being—had been—smashed.

"There," said Olly. She glanced up. The brown eyes behind the pink glasses became anxious. She caught a long strand of her hair and began to chew it.

Toby looked at her silently, as coldly as he could. He put hard glitters in his eyes—stab, stab.

"You don't like me."

"I don't like you," said Toby—smooth, sinister as a snake. Enigmatic. For heaven's sake, thought Toby. What was enigmatic?

"You don't like my ma," said Olly, hurt.

"Right," said Toby. "I don't *need* you."

17

"Your father needed us. I *love* your father. I never knew mine. . . ."

Toby pulled open a drawer and pulled out a photograph.

"*That* was my mother," he said.

Olly blinked seriously at the photo.

"She's beautiful," she said. "But she was young then, wasn't she? My mum was beautiful when she was young."

"Hah," Toby made a disbelieving snort.

"She was! Anyhow it's what's inside a person that makes them beautiful or not. So she still is, in a way."

"You must have some pretty funny things inside you then," said Toby.

"You know what you've got inside you?" said Olly, suddenly cut. "A nasty cold little toad, all alone on a cold little lily pad."

The truth hit Toby with a stinging slap. It was too near for comfort. He felt like that toad, cold and resentful on his solitary lily pad. All the other fish in the pond swimming around enjoying themselves—yak, yak, yak to each other. . . .

Olly backed away toward the door.

"All I came in for," she said, "was to ask you if you've got that essay. It's a reasonable thing to ask—all the schools are doing it, Miss Greiber said. There's a special section—"

Toby stepped forward.

18

"All right. I'm going," she said. And then, very softly, "T-o-a-d."

The door shut as the book hit it. Rage came and seethed in Toby. He wanted to smash something—anything. Instead he dropped a satisfactory blot over his homework, and ground it in.

He stared at the photograph of his mother. He didn't remember the real her at all—all he had was the piece of pasteboard, with her image black and white on it. Dying like that. Leaving him.

The blot had taken on the image of an owl—large eyes, cruel beak, tufted ears of feather. Toby chewed his lip and stared.

Maybe owls would make a good subject. Miss Hazell had announced it—an essay to be written on some animal or bird or insect. All the schools in the area were to take part.

"Wouldn't it be nice if our school"—Miss Hazell clasped her hands and beamed—"if your school could have one of the winners? Think of that."

"What sort of animals, miss?"

"Would our dog do?"

"I don't know any animals."

Miss Hazell stemmed the tide. She knew how. She had had long-enough practice. Soft she might look, but speak out of turn—really out of turn—and you were in trouble, faster than light.

"Shsh." It was the snake's command.

"Now. Let us see. As it's in aid of the World Wildlife Fund, I think it must be 'wild' life. And rare, preferably."

"Like steak," said some wit, who tried to bury himself fast under his desk as the glance caught him.

"What is rare, miss?"

"Dictionaries."

Banging of lids. Rustle of pages.

"Uncommon. Seldom seen. Unusual. Not many of them. Comparatively few."

"Enough. We now *know* what rare means. I want something from everyone—everyone."

Her glance rested on Toby. She hadn't missed the change in him.

"This is just up your alley," her look said. "Pull yourself together and do it."

"What's this essay business?"

Toby's father looked up from his book. His glasses had slipped as usual down his nose, leaving the red mark behind.

"You don't want to know," said Toby.

"I'm asking."

Toby eyed him. Identical pairs of blue eyes met. Toby grimaced and grinned. They were alone. No Olly. No Ma. Warmth returned.

"It's something I could do," Toby began.

His father let the paper drop and listened, nodding.

"Make it a proper study—scientific observation—not mushy and sentimental—'There are fairies at the bottom of our garden.'"

"Are there indeed?" It was her.

"We're talking about this competition essay," said Toby's father.

"Go *away*. Go away," thought Toby, so hard it hurt.

"Oh, that. Olly's been burbling about it. But you know that isn't the sort of thing she can do. *You* could, Toby," she added kindly.

Toby looked at her. She was humoring him, he decided.

"Yes, I could," he said.

And he would. He'd show them—all. Taking the thought with him, he went to bed. Waiting for sleep to come, he gnawed tentatively at the ideas that came and went—none of them right.

Toby sighed, hitched the blankets up over his shoulders. His eyes closed.

Chapter Three

Saturday was full of frost. Not the picture-book Jack Frost sort. Black and freezing.

Outside people were scurrying from point to point, with the least time wasted. By the afternoon, the doors were shut. All had retired to their lairs, eating, watching television, and looking out every now and then.

"Thank goodness we're inside."

Toby's house was a warm haven too. Much warmer than it had been. Ma had seen to it that the heating system had been fixed. For all her bulk, she didn't like the cold. Nor did poor Olly.

Nose streaming, pale hair dead and lank loitering around her face, she looked the picture of misery.

"Dod cub dear be," she said.

"I've no intention of coming near you," said Toby, truthfully. "You look awful."

"I do," Olly agreed. "I feel awful too."

"Poor old Olly," said Ma, "how about a hot lemon-ade?"

"And a game of chess," said Toby's father.

"I dod do how to play," said Olly sadly.

"I'll teach you—unless Toby—"

Toby's father took a quick look at him, inquiringly. Toby shook his head. He wasn't going to teach her chess; he couldn't imagine a worse fate. Why, imagine having to go over and over the pieces with her, then the moves, and then . . .

His father got out the wooden box and the board. He didn't look at Toby again. On either side of the fire, he and Olly bent over the pieces.

The rumbling protestations seething in Toby's throat died away before he had even the satisfaction of voicing them. Fury washed up and down in him like a bitter sort of tide. Chess was something he and his father did—had done. He couldn't even count the times they had played.

He wandered into the kitchen. Ma was there, kneading pastry.

"Cooking—the only thing to do on a day like this. My mind just turns to food," she said. "You wouldn't like to grease the pan for me?"

"Well, actually . . ." Toby thought of all the other more important things he had to do—of course he had something more important, more necessary, more essential—for heaven's sake, what was it?—to do.

23

"Never mind," Ma said quickly, before he could answer. "I'll manage."

Like a spare part, thought Toby. Suddenly decided, he pulled on his thick green parka and boots.

"Going out?" said Ma, blinking with amazement.

"Dod going out?" Olly.

"Going somewhere?" said Toby's father.

Toby stood there, hair spiked, his eyes wild.

"Yes. Yes. And yes. I—am—going—out."

He went into the passage, waited confidently for them to change his mind. Not that he would. Enough of that hot home-grown atmosphere. Out into the cold.

The door opened. *Was* it cold? Toby's nose numbed itself on the spot. He could see it out of the corner of his eyes, pink and pathetic. Nasty thing to be a nose, stuck right there out front.

No one stirred, no one called. Toby took his cold nose defiantly into the wastes. He shuddered. Suddenly, the idea hit him, warming him with a purpose. He turned to the woods.

The competition essay still wasn't done—true, Toby had won the prize often enough.

"First—Toby Grant."

"Well done, Toby—" he imagined his father saying.

"I'm amazed—and pleased—you *have* done well," that was Ma.

"Imagine you, first"—sighs—"you *are* clever," from Olly.

And so on and so on. The only thing was—that blank page, waiting for the first words of the masterpiece, was still unmarked. Inspiration, that's what he needed —and didn't he know that tracking in snow or frost was the easiest way to find an animal's hole.

Marks of claw and pad were scattered on the frozen ground all right. The air had a peculiar tingling silence in it. Toby pushed his way through the icy trees—lone wastes of Alaska, and he a solitary figure battling against the icy maelstrom, malstrom, male—oh, forget it, whatever it was that was cold and horribly unpleasant.

Toby narrowed his eyes into explorer's slits. If he was to find something rare, he would find it in the middle of the woods. Suddenly he had the oddest feeling of being watched. He stopped. Nothing.

Toby chewed his lip. The thought of going back seemed suddenly more pleasant and inviting. But then he saw them—the tracks. They were impossible tracks, like a man's, only enormous. Thoughts of the Abominable Snowman crossed his mind. He shuddered. Hot on the shudder came a thought. Toby smiled.

"I've written about the Abominable Snowman, Miss Hazell."

"Have you, dear boy, how nice. Such a rare animal."

"He's an interesting Abominable Snowman, Miss Hazell. He eats little girls."

"Does he, dear; what a strange habit."

25

"Especially ones called Olly."

"Oh well, but of course, that goes without saying. . . ."

Toby followed the tracks, and the trees closed behind him. The path was overgrown. He had never been this far in the woods. He took a quick, casual glance behind him and whistled aloud in a carefree sort of way.

Then the tracks stopped. Just like that. They led right up against a clump of blackthorn, a sort of thicket.

A sudden movement in the dense undergrowth made the hair prickle on the nape of Toby's neck. He turned to run—a roar sounded. A human roar.

"Rotten thing," said a voice.

An old oil lamp, still flaming, came hurtling over the bushes and fell on the iron-hard ground, shattering its glass. Still poised for flight, Toby looked in that direction. Sounds of muttering. Curses. Swaying of the twigs and creepers, which bound up the spot like a secret cocoon.

Almost as if the trees gave birth to it, the butterfly emerged—a strange butterfly—it was shrouded in coats, with a battered felt hat pulled down low over the eyes. The feet were booted and bound over with rags, held together with string. Gray hair fell down on either side of the face and straggled on into a beard.

The figure shuffled toward the light and bent over it.

It was still red-hot. With a muffled curse, the figure jerked back from the metal.

"Ooh-ah," it said, blowing on its murdered fingers. "Oooh."

Toby moved. The figure froze. Then it turned slowly. Two innocent blue eyes looked out under the eaves of hair.

Toby dredged up an uneasy smile and offered it.

"Good afternoon."

For heaven's sake, for heaven's sake—"Dr. Livingstone, I presume"—and you say "Good afternoon." Toby tried again.

"It's cold, isn't it?"

The blue eyes lit up.

"Arthur?"

It was a question, more than a question—a sort of hopeful statement.

"Not you, Arthur?"

Toby said nothing.

"Come out of the cold, boy."

The figure turned and shuffled away back into the thick undergrowth, where Toby could now see a faintly discernible path. The light was beginning to fade. A sort of unease took hold of him—but he followed.

"Curiosity killed the cat," thought Toby. "What *am* I doing?"

But then, surprisingly, they were through the worst

of the bushes, and there it was—the lair, as Toby thought of it. It was put together with care, from wood and branches and interwoven evergreen. Toby ducked his head and followed inside. There, the twin of the oil lamp was burning, faintly lighting the green gloom. The back extended into a small hill, dug out of the sandstone, like a cave.

The figure was bent over an old box. Scrabble. Scrabble. It turned.

Wire-framed glasses now hung on the nose and through them the blue eyes peered, first hopeful, then flat with disappointment.

"Hey. Hey. What's this now? You're not Arthur."

"I never said I was," pointed out Toby. "You did."

"You followed."

There was nothing strange or alarming now in the figure. He was just an old tramp with a hideout.

"You said, 'Come out of the cold,' " said Toby.

"No right to follow me here. It's my place. My place."

Toby looked around.

"Gosh, yes," he said. "And it's terrific. It's really neat."

"Neat. Terrific," the old man said suspiciously.

"Good. Great," said Toby. "And really clever, how it's all hidden. I bet nobody knows you're here."

Toby felt a wave of envy. Here was a retreat indeed. Everywhere he turned, his eye fell on signs that this was a permanent home. There were shelves lashed among the branches, and each shelf held spoils—mushrooms drying, fir cones, lumps of peeled wood, plants strung upside down—a few books, so thumbed and battered they looked on the verge of collapse. There were pots and pans, blackened by soot. There was a calendar—

"Hey, your calendar is a year old," said Toby.

The old man was looking bewildered.

"Not that it matters," added Toby hastily. "I think you've got a great place."

The old man sat down on one of the wooden box seats, shaking his head.

"I'm sorry I wasn't Arthur," said Toby awkwardly, "perhaps he'll come another time."

"No." The old man sat staring into the low embers of what had been a fire.

Toby shivered. The lateness of the hour and the silent stillness of his companion unnerved him. Slowly, as if he were emerging from a sleep, the old man looked up again. Looked this time. At Toby.

"Cold?" he said.

Toby nodded.

"This'll warm you." He blew on the embers and piled up dry twigs. "Sit down."

Toby sat meekly and watched. The blundering bear of a figure was nimble in the confined space of his own quarters. The kettle was shaken, with apparently successful results, and put on the fire. Tea was ladled into an old brown teapot with the spout half broken, sugar heaped into two chipped cups.

Toby suppressed a yelp as the cup of scalding tea was shoved into his hand—he, who never touched the stuff at home, sipped the thick, black brew.

The old man sipped and eyed him, and something that might have been a rusty smile creaked across the whiskers.

"Good, eh?" he said. "Good tea is food."

It was good. Like fire eating its way to his cold places. Places that had been cold for some time—even the thinking places, which were like cold toads on cold lily pads. Toby didn't feel like a cold toad any more.

"You like it?"

Toby nodded, truthfully, then feeling something else was called for, introduced himself.

"I'm Toby Grant."

It sank in slowly, the introduction. Then the old man cleared his throat.

"Josh Penfold," he said.

"Introduction over," thought Toby. "Now what?"

But Josh got up suddenly and began to take off his coat. There was another coat underneath, all belted with braided string, and under that a jacket. Slowly the large, lumbering bear of a man became smaller.

Josh sat down again, rubbing his hands with satisfaction as the flames burned brighter.

"Ah," he said. "That's all right, that is. It's worth being cold to be warm again."

"Do you—actually—live here? I mean, all the time?"

Josh looked around cautiously, then at Toby. He laid his finger along his nose and laughed—a clear, gay laugh—then he nodded.

"Gosh!"

Toby's eyes wandered around again. "You've got enough here for an army," he said. "It's a first-class hideout."

The smile faded from Josh's face.

"Home," he said. "Not a hideout. My home."

"Oh, yes," said Tony hastily. "But, oh, boy, private. No one could get at you here."

Josh considered him.

"People getting at you?" he said.

Toby nodded. "And how."

"Runaway?"

"No," said Tony, half regretfully. "Nothing like that. In fact, I think I better be getting home now."

Josh nodded. "Go on, then." Then, as Toby hesitated: "What are you waiting for?"

"Don't ask me," thought Toby. He didn't know what it was that drew him to this green hide—sorry, home—in the woods.

31

"Can I come again?" he blurted out.

Josh was already busy, scattering some crumbs of bread—

"Eh?" he said. He looked up from the two robins, who had flown down and were feeding by his feet. "All right. No one else. You."

"Thanks. Thanks." Toby ran back in the sweet cold semidark. A secret! A marvelous discovery, the old man of the woods.

With his face glowing, he crashed back into the house.

"You're back. We were getting worried."

Toby grinned benignly at her. Ma blinked.

"Where hab you been?" snuffed Olly. "Had you dead and buried."

Toby's father came to the kitchen door. "Wanderer returned," he said. "Thank the Lord. I'm starving."

It was Toby's favorite—macaroni and cheese, bubbling hot, golden and crispy.

"Where've you *been?*" said Olly again.

"Tracking in the woods," said Toby.

"Tracking!" said Olly. "In the woods!"

"You don't *have* to repeat it all," said Toby, smiling in the way calculated to prove the most infuriating. "That's what I said. For the essay."

"Oh, that," Olly lost interest. "You'd never find anything on a day like this to write about."

"Did you find anything—out of the ordinary, I mean?" asked his father.

The golden germ of an idea hit Toby.

"I might have."

"Tell," demanded Olly.

Toby bent his head over his plate.

"Not something likely," he said.

"Toby!"

Toby looked sideways at Ma.

"I'm quoting," he said, virtuously. "From George Bernard Shaw, actually."

Ma suppressed a grin, but not quite.

"If we all started quoting," said Olly, "we'd end up being arrested. I know some quotations—"

"We don't want to hear them," said her mother quickly.

"It's a secret." She was making a statement.

"It's a secret." Toby agreed.

Olly eyed him through her glasses in a considering way.

"You should do it more often, Toby Grant," she said. "It suits you."

Toby felt an unaccustomed wave of magnanimity overtake him. "*You* don't look quite so awful now," he said.

Afterward, getting ready to go to bed, Toby stared

33

out into the dark, past his own reflection, spike-haired, clean and pajama-ed. He could see in his mind's eye the hidden spot in the woods, where a strange old man was alone, but not lonely. The thought of him, like a small nut snug in its kernel, warmed Toby.

He remembered the burned hand. Next time he would take some ointment, a bandage, perhaps. On soft feet he padded into the bathroom. The medicine cabinet gave a loud click as he opened it.

"All right?" his father called up.

"Ears like bats," thought Toby, grinning.

"Headache," he lied. "Only a little one."

White lies, half-truths, he was becoming quite proficient. They were small victories in the war he seemed to be waging alone.

Toby took the ointment for burns, and some bandages. The cupboard was tidy. It was always so these days. He carefully moved a few things around. Serve her right if she got shaving cream instead of deodorant.

"Tomorrow," thought Toby, "or the next day, I'll go again." He hugged the thought. "I'm going to lie awake and work it all out—scientifically, a scientific study, a —for goodness' sake, wasn't there another word he could use?" A yawn engulfed him. "Tomor——"

Chapter Four

Returning wasn't so easy. For a moment's panic, Toby thought he had lost his way and would not ever be able to find the place again.

"In summer it must be completely hidden," he thought as he thankfully found the path he remembered. Toby looked around cautiously. He wouldn't have put it past Olly to try and find out where he was going. It wasn't that she was nosy—she was just, well, sort of interested in a morbid way.

"Going out?" she had said.

"Mmm."

"With me?" hopefully.

"Nope."

"Oh."

"One up for me," thought Toby. He looked at her under his eyelashes and dismissed a feeling of being sorry for her by lashing out.

"Isn't it possible, just faintly possible that you could find *something* to do other than gawking at me?"

"I don't gawk," said Olly. "I observe."

"Call it what you like. It looks like good old-fashioned gawking to *me*."

Olly gave a long, deep sigh and sucked her hair.

"All my life, all my life," she said, "I thought how nice it would be to have a brother—or a sister—but I really wanted a brother. Now, I've got one." She eyed Toby with distaste.

"I didn't ask you to come and live here," said Toby. "I've told you. I don't *need* you, or anyone."

"You're lying," said Olly. "But you don't know it," she added hastily, as Toby swung around.

Toby found the thicket again. A sudden feeling of awkwardness overtook him. He gave a loud, nervous cough.

"Er . . . Mr. Penfold," he called in a hoarse whisper. "Are you there?"

Silence.

"I'll look like a real nut," thought Toby, "if I'm not in the right place."

"Hello," he called. (I say. I say. I say. Hello. Hello. Hello.)

Toby wondered whether to make his way through uninvited, but it seemed rather like using someone's back door. He stood uncertain.

The bushes crinkled apart and a hand beckoned. "C'mon in then."

Toby went through. There was no friendly greeting. Josh eyed him suspiciously.

"Brought anyone?"

"No, of course not," said Toby indignantly. "I said so, didn't I? I haven't told a soul."

He held out the ointment and bandages.

"I brought these, though."

Josh took them and began to fumble with them.

"Here, let me. I've taken a first-aid course." Toby put on the ointment.

"Say!" Toby looked at the puffy, blistered hand. "Gosh," he said. "This will hurt."

Down among the beard, a smile began to start.

"I've had worse," said Josh, grinning now. "I won't die from it."

He nodded with satisfaction when the bandage had been put neatly in place.

"Good hand. Good hand," he said, as if he were speaking to a dog. "Can't have you getting sick. You're all I've got."

The same carefree laugh spun out again suddenly. It drew answering smiles from Toby.

"Think I'm mad?" said Josh.

"No. Of course not." Toby was always polite to strangers.

"I'm only mad Nor-nor West," said Josh.

"That," said Toby, "is Shakespeare."

"Surprised you," said Josh, with satisfaction. He crossed to one of the shelves and reached down a book.

"Works of William Shakespeare," he said. "All that was left. . . ."

"Left from what?"

Josh's eyes came back from the far distance.

"Eh? Never you mind." He glanced again at his hand. "One good turn deserves another."

He drew out a can from one of his boxes. It rattled. He opened it and peered inside. The can was a round one, once containing candy, which still remained in picture form on the outside, though faded and worn.

The lid snapped shut again. Something as smooth as a nut and about the same size was pressed into his hand. Toby opened it.

A tiny carved mouse, whiskers and claws minutely shaped, crouched in the palm of his hand. It was made of beechwood, smooth polished.

"Hey—that's marvelous," said Toby. "It breathes."

"The real one does," said Josh, indicating a place at the side of the wall.

Toby looked around enviously. "You've got the perfect hide—I mean to see animals," he added hastily, remembering Josh's objections before.

"I'm not lonely," agreed Josh. "There's the mice and the squirrels. There's the rabbits—and birds, the whole book of 'em—and stoats and voles. Sometimes I get a badger. There's a set down the way."

"Do you carve them all?" said Toby.

"Most—me and him," Josh pulled out a worn knife and snapped open the blade. He caressed the blade lovingly. "Sharp," he said. "Perfect sharp."

"You could sell them," said Toby. "People pay money for this sort of thing."

"When I want money," said Josh, "I do odd jobs—farms and that. I'll not sell these." He tapped the can.

A bird flew down and began to excavate for insects, just past their feet. A long, companionable silence followed, while Toby and Josh watched. It was the forerunner of many such moments in the next week or two.

February wasn't everyone's idea of walking weather, luckily for Toby. It made it that much easier to go, unseen, to visit Josh. He protected his secret like a mother bird her eggs.

Olly was nearly driven mad. "I know you're up to something," she said.

Toby practiced his new uninvolved face.

"Do you?" he said, blandly. "Goody for you."

Olly came closer.

"Your breath smells oniony," she accused. "We haven't *had* onions."

Toby remembered the stew, rabbit and vegetables and a touch of wild garlic.

"School dinner—" (it had been fish and chips) he said, with inspiration.

39

Olly was balked. "It's not that I'm—" she began.

"Not that you're nosy," Toby finished for her—
"B-boom."

"I'll do your math homework for you," she offered
brightly.

Toby got up. He took her shoulders—surprisingly
thin—and shook them.

"Look you—you mathematical genius—I don't *need*
your help. I don't *want* your help. Just because you've
come to live in our house doesn't mean I want you in
my hair all the time. Get it?"

Olly pushed her glasses up, but stood her ground.

"You've got a complex," she said, and quoted: "*I love
nobody, and nobody loves me.*"

It was close to the mark. Toby had developed an
increasing admiration for the independent life led by
Josh.

Toby used the rudest word he knew.

Olly's eyes widened. "Hey," she said. "You'll get it,
if they hear you."

Toby said it much, much louder.

Ma loomed into sight.

"Toby! For goodness' sake. Watch your language."
Toby eyed her.

"It expresses exactly how I feel," he said.

A smile began in the top of Ma's face but wasn't
allowed to reach her mouth.

"I often feel like that," she said. "But I control it."

40

She put her hand on his shoulder and shook it gently.

"Try it sometime," she said. Then she went into the bathroom and could be heard cleaning the tub.

Olly watched her mother's bulk disappear. Her brown eyes shone with love.

"Good old Ma," she said.

Watching her disturbed Toby. He didn't want to imagine other people having feelings. He turned.

"All right. I'm going," said Olly hastily.

Next time Toby visited Josh, his pockets were full.

"I've brought a piece of pie," he said. "Would you like it?"

Josh took the wedge politely.

"Thank you kindly," he said. "To tell you the truth I've a weakness for a good pie." He bit into it. "And very good it is too. Your ma's?"

Toby fidgeted—"Sort of," he said. "Stepma."

Josh's eyes gleamed sharply up through the hair.

"Arrh," he said reflectively. There was a pause. "Good pies she makes, does she?"

"I suppose so," said Toby reluctantly. "Well, yes—she's a good cook. But we managed before—" He stopped short.

Josh said nothing. He was a waiting pool of silence.

Toby began to talk. He talked for a long time. Then he stopped.

41

"I expect you think I'm stupid and ungrateful," he said.

Josh looked up. He considered Toby.

"No," he said. "But it seems to me you're wasting a lot of time wishing things were some way else. Time . . ." he shook his head. "Time never turns back. If you're not careful you can wish your life away. Took me a long time to work that one out. What's gone is gone. Enjoy the day."

Josh laughed, his strange, clear, ringing laugh. "Hark at Josh Penfold!" he said. "There you are, lad. I give it to you for what it's worth."

Toby smiled, but shook his head.

"If I were king of a kingdom like this"—he gestured to the woods—"I could do that too. It's people who mess things up. You knew that, or you wouldn't be a—" Toby hesitated. What on earth was the word between tramp and hermit? What was Josh anyhow?

Josh creaked up. His movements were sometimes jerky. He went and rummaged in a battered old knapsack.

Toby found himself looking at a photograph of a woman with a boy about his own age.

"My wife and son," said Josh. "Years ago. Arthur. That was Arthur."

"Did you . . . did you leave them?" Toby asked. "Curses," he thought. "Who's being nosy now?"

"They left me, in a manner of speaking." He sat down

42

again and stared out. He rubbed his hands together, as if suddenly chilled.

"One night in December—clear it was. We lived in London. Moon shining white on the roofs. I was on duty. Wartime, you see. Too old for the army, and a weak chest at that. Yes . . . it was really pretty that night. Emmy—my wife—always took Arthur down to the shelter. I had no worries. Siren sounded—off she'd trot, with Arthur and the cat in a basket and a thermos of hot soup. Pie too. Said good-bye—see you later—and that night it came—one of them doodlebugs. No warning, you see. Come out of the night, like something you dream about." He stopped and massaged his chest with his gloved hand.

Toby managed to sit quiet and ask no questions.

"Everything gone," said Josh, almost dreamily. "Sliced right through. No sign of nothing. No wife. No son. No home . . . Finished me. I did a little farm work. Then I cut loose. Started to wander. Been at it ever since."

"That's when *you* kept on wishing," said Toby.

Josh nodded. "That's when I kept on wishing; waste of time."

"All the same," said Toby. "It must be pretty good —to be free like you are. No ties. I'd like that."

Josh sat there, his hands hanging emptily in front of him.

"No," he said, finally.

"No?" Toby couldn't keep the astonishment out of his voice. "Why *not?*"

Josh got up and wandered shaggily around his small kingdom.

"Questions. Questions," he said testily, shaking his head, as if warding off buzzing flies. He glared at Toby.

Toby shifted under the glare. "Don't say anything else, you fool, he'll be even madder," he thought—but his eyes went on asking.

"People aren't meant to be islands," said Josh harshly. "I'm telling you. Now shut up. Don't keep on."

Toby buttoned his mouth meekly.

Josh got out his carving things. He looked up and grinned whitely at Toby.

"You'd better leave," he said. "It's time."

Toby got up reluctantly.

"Good-bye, Josh," he said.

Josh nodded, but didn't look up. The trees hid him from sight.

Ideas spun around in Toby's head so fast, they seemed like fireworks. He ran home, jumping up and grabbing the branches, now growing sticky with the promise of buds. Alive! Alive. Alive, alive ho!

Now he would do it. He was ready. He couldn't wait to put pen to paper. Essay, Essay—here I come. With a whoop, he tore into the hall.

"Oh," said Olly. "Mr. Red Indian, I presume."

Toby leaned over the banister and gazed at her as if she were under a microscope.

"You see the great author about to begin his work," he said. "Do not disturb."

Olly raised her invisible eyebrows.

"Don't worry," she said, sarcastically. "I wouldn't dare."

Toby raised his right hand and intoned,

"People—are—not—meant—to—be—islands."

He waited expectantly.

Olly's face glimmered up at him.

"Well—*I* knew that," she said.

Toby's hand fell. "You did? You would!"

"It's self-evident," said Olly, with care and some pride.

"What is?" said Ma, coming into the hall.

"I'm about to begin my essay for the competition," said Toby. "I don't want *anyone* interrupting."

"Well, all right," said Ma, reasonably. "We'll keep out of your way."

"The world waits, ha, ha," said Olly.

Toby closed his door with a bang. The sound thundered through the house. Toby considered. He opened the door. In a new, unused sort of voice, he said, "Er . . . sorry." Then he took a new sheet of paper—he uncapped the pen.

"Study of a Rare Animal," he wrote. Then he added "*Homo Solitarius*—The Solitary Man. . . ."

45

Chapter Five

You couldn't exactly see time going by—only the changes it brought.

Toby was growing. Each morning, the stretching, taller-than-before feeling. Painful in a way, but pleasing.

"Don't look *down* on me like that," said Olly, "under your eyelids."

Toby stretched himself even taller. "I can't help it if I'm growing," he said, with smug superiority. "Unlike some I could mention—I name no names, ha, ha."

Olly chewed her hair and looked at him through her glasses, looked up at him.

"Anyone would think you're doing it on purpose," she said. "It's just happening."

Toby shot his arms out of his cuffs as Ma came in.

"My shirts," he said. "Look at my shirts."

Ma looked aghast.

"Good grief," she said. "And your trousers. You'd

better have some new clothes."

"*I* haven't had anything new for years," complained Olly.

"Rubbish," said Ma kindly to Olly.

Olly sighed. "Oh well. It was worth a try. Can't you stop feeding him or something?"

"I'd like to see you try," said Toby, with a touch of the old belligerence.

But the truth was that the secret war he had waged against the new regime had palled. He found it quite difficult on occasions to stop himself from becoming absorbed in the family pattern. Besides, so much else was happening—newfound abilities at school, new interests. Days sped by so fast he hadn't got time to consider things. It was all happening.

"Grant for Mr. Weller. Grant for Mr. Weller."

"For heaven's sake," thought Toby, as the message was relayed to him. "*What* on earth?"

Mr. Weller was the principal.

"Hello, hello, hello," said his friend David, "what's our Toby been up to now?"

Toby shook his head. The bell clanged, announcing the beginning of break. He felt a nasty hollowness in the aby-abes-abyss—oh well, whatever it was—of his stomach. What on earth? Mr. Weller didn't see his class frequently. Toby had only met him a few times, and then he had been bolstered by others of his class.

"Rather you than me," said David.

Toby went along the corridor. One day, one day he supposed that smell of chalk and ink and rubber boats would seem to sum up his schooldays.

"Eeh, ah, I remember. I remember . . . when I was at school. . . ."

Toby let his bottom lip tremble and hunched along, tapping his invisible stick.

"All right?" said Miss Hazell, as she passed. "All right, dear boy!"

Toby jerked himself upright.

"Mmmah . . . yes," he mumbled.

Just lately, sounds and sights seemed extra vivid. He found himself looking at things, *really* looking. Even at Olly. She was a person. Different. And David too. Another—all marvelous and different.

The principal's door looked different too. Really it was the same brown varnish as any other door. The handle was, of course, polished brighter. The cleaning ladies saw to that.

"Make sure of the metal, dear, especially the principal's handle. Give that a good polish, won't you?"

Toby, curlers in his hair, broom in hand, pursed up his mouth and shuffled cleaning-lady-like up and down.

The door opened suddenly.

"Yes?"

Toby swallowed so suddenly and hard that it hurt.

"Mr. Weller, sir." His voice came out in a bright squeaky shout. "I mean, Mr. Weller, sir." Toby managed to lower his voice an octave. "You wanted me."

"I can't think why," said Mr. Weller, eyeing him with some distaste.

"I'm Toby Grant, sir. You sent for me."

The sandy eyebrows twitched over the black-framed glasses.

"Ah. Come in. Come in."

Toby slid himself through the door.

"Sit down."

Mr. Weller crossed to his chair. He folded his hands over the beginnings of a round stomach. He contemplated Toby.

"Ye-e-s," he said.

Toby eyed the contents of the desk with absorbed enthusiasm. Ruler. Blotter. In-Tray. Out-Tray. With an effort he raised his eyes. He felt himself growing again, his cuffs edging up—for heaven's sake, people'd be able to see soon. His feet elongated themselves—he tried to conceal them under the chair.

Like a conjuror producing a rabbit, Mr. Weller opened a drawer and drew out a sheaf of papers.

Toby recognized it.

Mr. Weller looked at it, then he looked at Toby again.

"Your essay," he said. "Very interesting. Very original. 'Rare animal' . . . hmm. But farfetched. Still, a

49

good effort. Best of those sent in . . . but, but, but . . . aha, now young feller-me-lad, this isn't all true, is it? Based on fact, they were supposed to be, you know."

What did the man mean? thought Toby. "It is true," he said.

Mr. Weller's jaw slackened, and his pipe lost its anchorage on his teeth. "What? True? Factual?" He leaned forward, tapping the pages. "You mean to tell me this old man of the woods really exists? Not made up?"

"Of course he does!" Toby was indignant now. "I don't write unscientific essays. It was a study. Of a rare animal."

Mr. Weller leaned back. "Ah, yes . . . your father . . . teaches biology, doesn't he, at the College. Married Mrs. Sands . . . that's right. . . ."

"Might as well not be here," thought Toby.

"That settles it." Mr. Weller stood up. "Congratulations, Grant. This will be our entry into the Area Competition from the school. Well done. I'll tell your . . . er . . . ah . . . your mother. Mmm. Mmmm."

Mr. Weller made dismissing gestures with his pipe. Toby, dazed and gratified, emerged into the corridor again.

He knew what he had written was good. Now he was proved. The famous author stalked down the corridors—plaques on the door of the classroom. "Toby Grant worked here—"

"Hey. Are you O.K.?" said David.

"The best in the school," said Olly dreamily. "You *are* clever."

Toby eyed her suspiciously. But she was looking at him with such pleased admiration that he relaxed.

"You're pretty good at math," he said magnanimously. "For a girl."

"Sex—actually—has nothing to do with it," Olly couldn't resist adding. "But just wait till they hear—Ma and Daddy. They'll be so glad."

"Daddy," thought Toby, but more with amusement than resentment. "How she reveled in it!"

"Can I *see* it? Can I read it?"

"You wouldn't understand it."

"Wouldn't I just? At least let me try."

"Oh . . . well. I've got a rough copy."

Olly took the papers and smoothed them with a grubby but reverent hand.

"Gosh," she said. Then she dipped her head and began to read.

They *were* pleased. Ma left Toby to tell his father.

Toby grinned. "Olly's reading the masterpiece now."

"Good boy. Well done! I'm glad you made the effort." Toby's father looked at him hard. He meant more than he said. And Toby knew. He and his father . . . they had sympathy—no, empathy—well, something or other "thy." They understood each other. Toby

51

turned a little red and shifted his feet about. "Aw, well," he said. "I meant to all along."

Olly came bursting in. Her face was pink. She flourished the essay.

"Well!" she said. "Of all the mean, low-down boys. To keep a thing like that secret! To think that's where you were going—you old so-and-so you."

"If I'd told you, you'd have been down there faster than an arrow, with a posse of friends. 'Come and see what I've got, yak, yak!' "

"I would not! I can be very dis-creet." Olly said.

Ma and his father followed the interchange from side to side, with smiles of amusement.

"Stop!" called Ma. "I'm beginning to feel I'm at Wimbledon. Peace, I say."

She folded her arms and eyed them both from her heavy-lidded eyes.

"Can we read it, Toby?"

"Yeah, of course." Toby handed it over. "At least you and Dad won't be down ferreting him out."

"Him?"

"Read it," said Toby confidently.

Later, when Toby came downstairs, bright-eyed, bushy-tailed, King of the Castle, his father greeted him.

"It's true, of course?" It was hardly a question.

Toby rolled his eyes. "Of *course* it's true! For heaven's sake, why does everyone keep on asking? I'll show you, if you like."

"Does he know?" It was Ma.

"He? Know what?" Toby, having expected instant glory, was angry. He stuck out his chin aggressively.

"Does this man know you've written about him? For a public competition?"

"Oh, yes. So likely. 'Excuse me, Mr. Penfold. I'm writing about you—scientific study, you know—of a rare animal!' Of course he doesn't know."

Toby's father and Ma exchanged glances.

"What's the *matter*?" said Toby. "I thought you'd be pleased. What are you—the something inquisition!"

"Toby," Ma said, automatically reproving.

"I didn't *say* it," said Toby. "I said 'something.' "

There was a brief silence.

"Yes. It *is* a very clever piece of work," Toby's father said. "It deserves to be entered from the school. But—didn't you think about this Mr. Penfold? What he'd feel? If he's a recluse, a solitary sort of person, won't he be angry?"

Toby cast about for the answer. He came up with nothing satisfactory. He hadn't actually thought about what Josh would think. He had used him.

Olly, still bursting for sympathy with Toby, jumped in—feet first.

"Rare animals are *protected*," she said. "So this Mr.

53

Penfold will be. There'll be notices around his nest, I mean, his lair—well, his home. 'Do not disturb!' Imagine giving him a Latin name." She rolled it around her tongue. "*Homo solitarius!* So I don't see how he *can* mind."

Even as she spoke, uncertainty began to advance over her face. She ranged herself alongside Toby, like a small skinny soldier. But her eyes, as she waited for Toby to confound them all, were anxious. She chewed her hair.

"Well," Toby's father tried to inject a lighter note. "He certainly may be left alone. He may even never hear of it. Let's hope so."

"You *told* me," said Toby, "to make my essay scientific—I did. I didn't think." His voice trailed away. "I didn't . . ."

"I think *you're* all simply horrible," said Olly. "Toby's gone and done this and all you can do is grumble at him."

Her sympathy made hot tears begin to rise at the back of Toby's throat. Aghast, he felt them coming on. He blinked furiously. But far worse was the feeling of guilt beginning in his own mind.

Toby glittered the tears into hard, stabby looks at his father and Ma.

"You just don't know *anything*," he said and, picking up the sheets of paper, he blundered out of the room.

Olly started to follow him, but Toby swung around. "Leave me alone," he snarled.

At school, it was different. Miss Hazell was delighted.

"Just think," she fluttered. "Out of all those essays. I *knew* you could do it." She hesitated, loath to miss improving the hour. "Mind you, your work of late . . ." She shook her head and her chins wobbled. "Very below standard. Never mind. Different now, eh?"

People who hadn't known he existed came and spoke to him.

"What did you *write* about?"

Toby couldn't resist it. He basked in the interest —even from the captain of the soccer team, who singled him out.

"Hey, Grant. I had a stab at that essay. What've you got that I haven't got?"

Toby looked up admiringly. "Brains?" he said.

"Fresh."

"Someone said you found an old man, living in the woods?"

Caution cooled Toby. He tried to change the subject. But they were at him, baiting him with doubts, compliments. . . .

"Tell. Tell."

And Toby told.

Chapter Six

"Out of all the schools in this area, we are very pleased to find one of our boys, Toby Grant, a winner in the World Wildlife Fund Essay competition. Congratulations." Mr. Weller paused, waiting for the applause from the Assembly.

He held up his hand. "The subject of his essay was 'The Solitary Man—'"

Surprisingly there were snickers from the lower grades. Mr. Weller fixed them with a cold, sandy-browed stare.

"This essay will receive a prize of ten pounds and will be published in one of the larger local papers."

Red from embarrassment and glory, Toby received his money. He couldn't wait to get home to tell his father. Ma knew already. He could see her, sitting at the side, hands folded impassively in her lap. Her brown eyes were hooded.

"Let her stew," thought Toby. He didn't need her approval.

Modestly, eyes cast down, he walked back to the classroom. See the famous writer—he passed a faint hand over his genius-laden forehead. "I knew him as a boy." In a manner befitting a prizewinner, he got out his work—

"Not English, you fool. Math," said David.

Toby descended to earth with uncomfortable rapidity.

All the same, all the same, the thought nagged at him. He'd better go down and see Josh. Explain it all. . . .

With unwilling steps, Toby took the familiar path. A rough notice nailed on a stick was stuck in the ground. On it was scrawled in chalk, "Here liveth a rare old bird."

Toby remembered the titters from the younger ones. They had smelled him out. Toby went on, mouth set.

"Danger. Wild animal lives here," said the next scrawl.

Toby's stomach felt cold. He longed to turn and go home—forget he had ever been there. But he went on, goaded, driven by the doubts—prejudices—of his father and Ma.

"Josh," he called. Small voice. Let him not be here. Please. "Er . . . Mr. Penfold."

A wild figure came out.

"Leave me alone you—" It stopped short. "Eh? Toby?"

"It's me," said Toby.

"Thought it was one of them little pests. Been on at me." A smile came, familiar, gay under the wild gray hair. "Thought you'd gone. Eh, lad. Come inside."

Toby followed. Judas. That's what it was. Judas-feeling. Ten pounds. Not pieces of silver.

"Sit down."

Already Josh was brewing the tea. He laughed.

"I've been a match for them, though." He nodded. "Frightened them to death. Came roaring out."

"It was me," Toby began. . . .

When he had finished, Josh was listening, mug of tea half suspended from his lips.

"A study. Of a scientific nature," he mouthed the words carefully. "Of me. A Solitary Man. A rare animal." He looked around, as if seeing it for the first time.

Then he began to make noises. Toby wondered with alarm if he was having a fit of fury, but the noise resolved into a shout of laughter. Josh slapped his leg.

"That's good. That's good." The laughter left him breathless. He rubbed his chest. "Eh . . . I never thought I'd be the subject of an essay."

Tell him, thought Toby. Tell him now about it being published in the paper. But the words didn't come out.

58

"You don't mind?" A smile of relief spread on Toby's face.

"Too bad if I did," said Josh—but he grinned as he said it. "Mind you," he added. "They annoyed me—the little nuisances. Shouting names at me. Things—but I see now, why. They'll get tired of it, leave me in peace."

Toby nodded, avoiding looking at him. After all they might never . . . old news was stale news. . . . Josh didn't read the paper.

Toby argued with himself. He convinced himself without much difficulty.

The air was mild. There was a feeling of spring stirring in the air. Josh had shed a layer of coat.

"Spring," he said, snuffing the air, like a connoisseur tasting wine. "Spring coming—"

"He didn't mind!" Toby burst out with it as soon as he saw Ma. "I told you. I went to see him. He laughed."

Ma's face lit up. "Why, she's dead pleased," Toby thought. "She really minded." He put the thought aside to chew over later.

"Oh, I'm *glad*, Toby," she said. "It would have spoiled it all if you had hurt the old fellow."

Toby grinned. "It'd hurt him a lot more if he heard you. 'Old fellow' indeed!"

Ma laughed. "Just the same," she said. "It's just as well to remember that other people have feelings, before you use them as a scientific experiment."

"Have you feelings?" Toby thought, eyeing the large bulk. He looked up. "Why, doggone it"—that was a marvelous expression—"she *has* too."

Suddenly embarrassed, Toby covered it up by playing the fool.

"Food. Food. Glorious food," he shouted, "food for thought. Food for a genius."

"Well, if it's only food for thought," said Ma, "you can have a sack of it right away. If it's food for any other part of your anatomy, you can have it in twenty minutes."

"I'll settle for that," said Toby.

That evening he had a visitor. The bell rang. Olly answered it.

"It's Miss—er—Gates—for you, Toby."

Miss Gates appeared. Time and fashion had passed her by. Her skirts were long and shapeless. Her hair was neatly cramped behind her ears in little rolls.

"If I might," she fluttered. "Just a word. So sorry to disturb you all. I felt I must—only a little while."

Toby's father had risen politely. "Did you want to see someone?"

"Toby Grant. If you could spare—I'd be so grateful —it's the Welfare, you know. I represent the care of our elderly citizens."

"Take the back room," said Toby's father, rolling his

eyes over to Toby. "Take Miss—er—Gates there."

Toby made hideous faces at this base desertion, behind the thin, angular back. But his father grinned and waved him away.

Miss Gates sidled out and into the back room.

"Mr. Weller—you see. He told me. So clever. I mean —the thing is—do you mind telling me—is he still there?"

"Who?" said Toby, deliberately obtuse.

"This—er—gentleman. In the wood. Poor man. Poor old man."

"He's not poor at all," said Toby. "He *likes* it there."

"So he is still there?" The eyes sharpened.

"Steady," thought Toby. "Think what you say."

"Might be," he said vaguely.

"Ah." Miss Gates sat back.

"Now, Toby," she said cozily. "It *is* Toby, isn't it? Can you tell me about your Mr. . . . . er . . . ."

Toby watched her flounder.

"He's all right," he went on repeating.

"Need of help? Need of care? What we're for. We look *after* our elderly citizens," rattled on Miss Gates.

"He's gone," said Toby suddenly.

Miss Gates mouth fell open. Toby watched it. Fishmongers, he thought of. On the slab. Gaping.

"Gone?" It was a gasp. Disappointment was there. "But you said . . . ."

"I made a mistake," said Toby, warming to his

theme. "I remember now, he told me. Off to see his cousin. In Australia." Steady. Steady. That was a bit farfetched. Suspicion sharpened the eye of Miss Gates.

"No, no—not Australia. Somerset or somewhere."

"I see." Miss Gates clipped her tones. "I see. I'll trouble you no longer then." She got up, clasping her bag like a shield with both hands.

Scarcely had she gone when Olly bounded in.

"I was listening," she said. "Oh, Toby. You lied."

"I had to," said Toby. "Josh won't want people like her around."

"But you lied *badly*," said Olly, impatiently. "Forget the morals. I'm talking of the performance. She's only got to read the news tomorrow and she'll *know*."

Toby clapped his hand to his head. "Gadzooks!" he cried. "All is lost."

Olly eyed him coldly. "Stop acting," she said. "You're not on stage."

Toby shrugged irritably. "Oh, shut up. Nag. Nag. Nag. A houseful of women. Yak. Yak. Whatever I do is wrong. It's wrong to tell the truth about the man, and it's wrong to lie about him. It's wrong to do *anything*. That old Miss Gates. She's just one of those committee women. Why, if she came face to face with Josh, she'd die of shock. His hair. His beard. He doesn't always smell too fresh either." Toby imitated Miss Gates smelling Josh.

Olly began to laugh.

Chapter Seven

The news broke.

"Headlines," gloated Olly, bent over the paper. "Middle-page headlines, anyhow," she added, the preciseness of her mathematical mind getting the better of her.

"If anyone asks," said Toby, "if you want to know, I won't tell them. Where he is, I mean."

"It's not a very big woods, Toby," said his father, busily eating his cereal.

"Actually," said Olly, making triangles with her brown sugar on the porridge, "actually it's seventy-two acres at least."

Toby looked at her gratefully.

"Yes. There," he said.

"That won't stop anyone, if they want to find him."

"No one found him before. Except me."

"But they didn't *know* he was there," said his father patiently. "It's knowing that makes the difference."

"Oh, let him finish his breakfast, John," said Ma. "It's his day of glory, after all. It looks good in print, Toby."

"Well—thank you," said Toby.

"Yes. Yes, of course." Toby's father touched him on the shoulder. "Congratulations, son. I'm proud. We all are."

A wave of embarrassment smothered Toby.

"Hey," he said, "I don't want speeches."

"No," said Olly. "You want flowers and hallelujahs. Allow me."

She pulled the heather out of the little pot, where it bloomed dryly, and presented it to him.

"You take it," she said.

Toby looked at her suspiciously, but she was serious. Toby bowed.

"Thank you, dear," he said gravely.

Then they both began to laugh. Ma joined in. Her shoulders heaved, and sound burst from her in sharp *ha, ha, ha*. Toby's father, eyeing them with mild astonishment, began to smile.

Ma caught sight of the clock.

"Good grief. Look at the time."

For the first time, Toby and Ma went to school together. Things were falling into place at last—Toby thought of Josh with gratitude. In a way, this was his doing. Without too much embarrassment, he walked past his friends, accompanied.

At the gate, a nod. Ma's old smile flashed out.

"See you later."

But by then, the reporter and the photographer had arrived. She didn't look like a reporter. She wore a red shiny hat and a tight blue-belted raincoat.

"Hello. You're Toby Grant," she started. "I've got a distant cousin in your class, I think. Know him? Peter Brown?"

Toby didn't know him. But by that time the reporter had come to the real point.

"About this old man," she said. "Do tell me a little more. I read your winning entry for the competition. Marvelous. Did it take you long?"

It was easy to start chatting about how long it had taken, how it came about. Gradually Toby drifted nearer to the heart of the matter.

"He wouldn't mind a teeny little photograph, would he? And you, of course."

Toby hesitated. The photographer took a flash shot of him. Toby grinned, a little bashfully—having your photograph taken by a newspaper reporter was something. . . .

"The famous something or other made his way to the plane, surrounded by eager photographers. Toby Grant—personality plus. Ha. Ha. . . ."

"I don't suppose he'd mind," he said aloud.

"We know more or less where he is," the reporter rattled on. "Just one point. Is it the left path from here into the wood?"

"No—the right and then left and left again and right and there's the thicket, by the side of the old quarry."

"Of course," she said, smiling. "Of course. Thanks a lot, Toby. Look out for your photograph in the *Daily Clarion*."

"The *Daily Clarion*," said Toby's father. "That rag! It's the worst sensation-monger of the lot."

"She seemed very nice," said Toby defensively.

"That's her job," said Toby's father. "It's the paper I'm talking about. Let's hope they don't find him. Short of news, I suppose. Can't have been any nice murders or spy trials lately."

Like a cold snail inside Toby wriggled the thought that he had given them directions.

"We'll have to wait until tomorrow to see the paper," said Olly. "I can't wait. Rag or not, we've *got* to buy it."

"Your money, then," said Ma placidly. "Not ours."

"I may remind *you*, Ma mine," said Olly, "that last week you had to rob my piggy bank to pay the baker because you couldn't find your purse. Now ninety-seven pence at six percent for one week . . . let me . . . see."

Ma rolled her eyes. "Good grief," she said. "I'll buy it. Don't slay us with mathematical formulas."

"Shsh," Toby's father was leaning forward, turning up the television, which was on the area news program.

"Bird watching is not usually in our reporter John McCrae's list of favorite activities, but today he made his way down into the heart of the Surrey woods, where a very strange and rare bird is believed to have nested. . . ."

There was a film showing some thick trees and John McCrae crouching, gazing through the binoculars. Then the bushes ahead parted and a figure came out.

"It's Josh," said Toby.

"Shsh."

"It would appear that, incredible as it may seem, Mr. Josh Penfold has lived here on his own for some years —and was only recently discovered when a schoolboy wrote an essay about him, a winning essay, for a local competition. The essay was about a rare animal and Mr. Penfold is rare indeed—a proper modern Mr. Robinson Crusoe. Mr. Penfold. Mr. Penfold."

Closely, revealing, the camera tracked up to Josh Penfold's lined and weatherbeaten face, surprised, bewildered . . . taken completely aback.

"Mr. Penfold," went on the smooth voice of John McCrae as he interviewed. "You're a very rare man. Can you tell us more about your way of life?"

Stumbling, hesitating, drawn out by clever ques-

67

tioning, Josh revealed himself with an innocent candor that exploded like a bomb into the living rooms of television viewers.

Toby's father, gray hair standing on end, watched intently and with growing concern.

"Oh, Lord! He's offering himself up on a plate."

Ma made soothing noises.

"Isn't he *sweet* and *super*," said Olly, intent on the screen.

But Toby was looking at Ma and his father.

"You mean they'll keep on writing about him?"

"They'll wring him dry—until some better news pops up. Then they'll drop him."

"For goodness' sake! They're only filming him. You act as if they're . . . murdering him!" Toby almost shouted. "Funny sort of people you are. I thought you'd be glad about it all. Other people think I was clever. Not you—you two." He glared at Ma.

His father looked at Toby. A long level look.

"There are other things beside cleverness," he said.

Olly looked at Toby's white face.

"I guess Josh Penfold will become a famous film star."

She put out a consoling hand and gave a quick stroke to Toby's shoulder.

Toby shrugged it off.

"Don't be *stupid*," he snapped. "You're just being childish."

"Actually," said Olly, hurt. "*That* is what I am—physically, although mentally I am somewhat superior to some I could mention who are at a much more advanced physical level."

"Don't stuff our heads with words," said Ma. "You're fogging the issue—though there's nothing we can do—but wait and see. . . ."

There wasn't long to wait and see. The next day Josh Penfold was news—and incidentally Toby Grant.

Interviews were arranged between them. Toby met Josh, again accompanied by a bevy of cameramen.

"Hi, Josh," said Toby shyly, "hope you don't . . ."

Josh looked like a bewildered child. All the bounce seemed to have gone out of him.

"Did you . . . did you . . . was it you told them where I was?" he got out at last.

Toby raised his eyes with difficulty to meet the blue eyes of Josh.

"Yes . . . but somehow . . . I didn't mean to."

Josh nodded.

"They keep on taking pictures. Mr. Robinson Crusoe, they call me." Josh laughed suddenly. "Mr. Robinson Crusoe."

With a hand faintly shaking, he produced the tattered newspaper cutting. "Look—it's all here. There was a lady, a man, and television cameras. Now they want to film me inside."

Josh jerked his head, indicating behind him.

"Oh, Josh!" Toby was aghast. The path into the green hidden thicket was clear—trampled by many feet. It would never be secret again.

Josh looked on. "I asked them," he said. "I asked them to be careful. They wanted special shots, you see."

"I wish I'd never written the essay," blurted Toby.

Josh managed to produce his old grin. "No good wishing—haven't I told you? What's happened has happened. Got to lump it."

Coming away from the woods, Toby was stopped by two grubby, giggly little girls. They thrust an autograph book in his hand.

"Sign it—please," they whispered, in high, hoarse voices.

Toby sighed. It was the same all the way—people stopping him, wanting to be seen talking to him. Boys who hardly knew him cycling past and calling casually, "Hi, Toby."

The warmth of being news spread over Toby. He felt ten feet tall and twice as important—he was someone. Lucky family to have such a member—he opened the gate and walked in, swaggering slightly.

Olly was sitting on the lower stair, absorbed in a book, chewing her hair. She didn't look up. Toby eyed her. Nothing.

"Well?" he said loudly.

Olly looked up. Far, far away.

"Hello," she said, unseeing.

"You look revolting chewing that hair," said Toby.

Olly removed it. "Mmm," she agreed. "Trying to give it up."

"*I've* been interviewed. And filmed. Some people asked for my autograph."

"Did they?" Olly came to slowly, far too slowly.

"Yes . . . you know . . . little book. Sign, please."

"All right," said Olly. "Good. Bully for you. But don't keep on about it. I've got to the most exciting story in my book—and I've got to get it read before I start my homework."

Toby trailed into the living room and threw his coat down.

"Pick that coat up," said Ma, coming in.

Toby eyed her. Ma looked back equably.

"I was going to," he said ungraciously, snatching it up.

"Red carpets. Ha. Ha," thought Toby, as he went up to his room. Talk about no prophet being famous in his own country—if he'd written that essay when it was just him and Dad—they'd have celebrated. Would he have written it? Secretly? Like that? That was to show her—rub her face in it. Not her clever Olly—him. He had won it.

Toby skipped away from the reasons that had made

71

him write. Depression rolled in clouds on him. He stared out of the window.

What was Josh doing now in his ruined lair? "All my fault," thought Toby. It was a hideous thought. He banished it quickly. Get through the day. Tomorrow would surely bring something different.

Chapter Eight

Tomorrow did. Yesterday's news was dead news. To the relief of Toby, tinged only with the faintest regret, things slid back to normal.

One last visit, thought Toby, just to set the record straight.

He went down the familiar path. He hadn't gone far when Olly joined him.

"I'm coming," she said flatly.

"O.K." Toby was indifferent now. A secret was no more. It was difficult to think how it had remained hidden so long—even though the green haze of spring was beginning to mist and cloud the turnings.

They found Josh sitting in a clearing, carving. He looked up apathetically.

"Oh. It's you."

"And me," said Olly, gravely. "How do you do, Mr. Penfold. I've been very anxious to meet you. I'm Toby's stepsister."

Josh put down his knife, wiped his hand down the side of his trousers and shook her hand.

"Miss," he said.

"Olly. Call me Olly."

"Olly."

"That's beautiful." Olly picked up the nearly finished carving. It was an owl, squat and feathered, with beak and large socket eyes. Olly hung over it, tinsel hair falling down either side of her face, lips parted over the tombstone teeth.

Josh smiled.

"You shall have it," he said. He chuckled. "Didn't tell Them," he said. "Keep some things to myself."

"You'll be able to go back to normal now," said Toby.

A hunted look came over Josh's face. "A Miss Gates," he said. "She's been here. Welfare or something. Coming back."

"Oh, her!" said Toby.

"You know her?"

Toby made a face.

Josh grinned whitely in his beard.

"I see you know her. Wants to put me in some old people's home."

"Elderly citizens," corrected Toby.

"Ah, that was it," said Josh. "Had me coming and going, she did, with her talk."

He rubbed his chest with his knuckles and got up stiffly.

"Mr. Penfold?"

Toby and Olly flanked Josh and turned to face the new intruder.

Josh sighed like a beaten man. "Aye," he said limply.

P. C. Williams, fresh-faced and uneasy, cleared his throat.

"Mr. Penfold," he said. "These woods are the property of the Borough. We cannot allow unauthorized camping here. Therefore I am instructed to give you notice to quit within three days." P. C. Williams, having delivered his message officially, relaxed. "Very sorry, Mr. Penfold, sir. But you see how it is. If they allow you here, every Tom, Dick, and Harry will be along with their things."

"Camping," said Josh. "I'm not camping."

"He's got his *home* here," said Olly.

"Well, he shouldn't have, miss. It's not allowed."

"He can't just *move* everything," said Toby.

P. C. Williams began to flounder. This was out of his depth.

"I've told you," he said doggedly.

"Do I get a word in?" said Josh.

Olly and Toby and P. C. Williams looked at him.

"When people have finished taking pictures of me, filming me, writing about me and telling me where I

75

can't stay, perhaps someone would tell me where I *can* go."

"Haven't you any relatives . . . ?" began P. C. Williams.

"Don't start *that* again." Josh shook his head, like a bear, baited. "That Miss Gates. She's done all that."

A smile of relief spread across the stubby, pink features of P. C. Williams. "Ah," he said. "Of course— Miss Gates will fix you, sir. She's the Welfare. She'll fix you."

"Aye. I was afraid of that," said Josh.

"You could come home with us," said Olly, taking Josh's large calloused hand into her own skinny paw. "My ma would be pleased."

Josh looked at Olly, and his eyes burned soft blue, "Thank you, my maid," he said.

"Yes. Go on. Why not," said Toby.

Josh shook his head.

"No," he said. "It wouldn't do. Welfare is different. If I have to, Welfare isn't charity. I learned that in the war."

"Shall I get in touch with her?" P. C. Williams said, all eager.

Josh grinned. "No need," he said. "Her'll be back soon enough. Reckon she's got me marked down."

P. C. Williams put on his helmet, touched it, and strode away.

"You're a fat-al-ist," said Olly, seriously.

"I suppose I am," said Josh.

"You don't have to stay for long," said Toby. "When you find somewhere else . . ."

"Not for long."

Toby felt suddenly that it was Josh reassuring him.

"Well, then—"

"Well, then—"

"Wherever you are, Mr. Penfold," said Olly, "I will come and see you. Truly I will."

Josh nodded.

"I'll have him ready," he said, touching the half-finished carving. "When you come."

Josh moved into the thicket—"Best get ready," he said. "I travel light."

On their way back, Olly was unusually silent. Toby glanced at her sideways.

"He's like something out of a poem," she said at last.

"*The old man's shape and speech—all troubled me. I seemed to see him pace . . . continually,*" quoted Toby, with conscious virtuosity.

"Toby Grant." Olly stopped in her tracks, teeth glinting. "You amaze me. You *really* amaze me. Sometimes you seem almost feeling."

"I'm not a sloppy sentimentalist like you," said Toby.

"Sentimental. What *is* sentimental? Feeling? Emotions?"

"Spare me the dictionary," said Toby.

Olly looked at him with understanding.

"He'll be all right," she said. "These places are very nice now. He's brave—he can take it."

"He won't be lonely," said Toby eagerly.

"No."

"He'll have better food."

"Yes."

"Only for a little while."

"We'll visit him."

Toby kicked the last pangs of conscience away.

"Home!" he cried. "Charge!"

"Let's bake a cake," said Olly, panting along behind him. "Take it to him."

"With a file inside. Whoops!" Toby let out pent-up feelings and leaped up at the new leaves.

Chapter Nine

There were no bars at Pinewood. The town was proud of its home for elderly citizens.

Fresh, clean, bright—a model of its kind, so everyone said. The city council regarded getting into Pinewood on a par with entering heaven. There was a garden, with flowering shrubs, television in the lounge, and every citizen had a room of his own. "Think of that," said the relatives, as they thankfully discharged their burdens into its doors. "Lucky, lucky you."

Lucky, lucky Mr. Penfold, with a last write-up in the paper, was received into its portals. Everyone sighed with relief, patted each other on the back, and watched thankfully as the ripples died away.

Soon the leaves would cover the place where he had lived. Soon the dampness would bring the shelves rotting to the floor. Soon the animals and birds would learn to look for food elsewhere. Soon Mr. Penfold, that rare animal, would adapt himself and become indistinguishable from the other elderly citizens. . . .

Toby had mixed feelings on visiting day. What on earth should he wear? He'd never been to Josh's without boots and a heavy jacket. Did one dress up, or what?

"Hello. I'm coming," announced Olly.

"You're not," said Toby flatly.

Olly came into full view. She *had* dressed for the occasion in her new red dress.

"What on earth! You look like something off a Christmas tree," said Toby.

Olly looked down, unease appearing behind her glasses.

"I do?"

Toby nodded. "Last year's Christmas tree," he added nastily.

Olly looked up, getting mad, but then she saw the mixed clothing strewn around Toby's room.

"Oh, pooh, you only say that because you don't know *what* to wear."

"What about the pale blue today, sah, or shall we have the sky-blue-pink," she said, mincing across the room.

Toby bit in a grin. "I shall wear my school clothes," he announced, with thankful decision.

"Slumming it," said Olly.

"And I shall go alone," said Toby, pushing her out.

"But—"

"Alone."

Olly's wail was cut off by the door. Then came Ma's voice. "Alone today. Quite right. Good grief, he doesn't want an army visiting him . . . no, I know you're not an army—but sometimes you seem like an awful lot of people, Olly. Toby today. Next time you too."

Toby opened the door. Seriously he said, "Thanks."

Ma nodded and made a dignified journey into the kitchen. She poked her head around the door.

"Oh—there's the cake. It's in the pantry. The one with nuts on. Take it."

Toby and Olly's cake had ended in disaster, thin and flat with little burned currants studding it.

"Who would have thought it was so difficult to make?" Olly had sighed.

"Or that you could produce such a revolting-looking object," said Toby.

"You weighed it out," said Olly.

"You mixed it," said Toby.

"There's one thing, for sure," said Toby's father, coming in and surveying the object with horror. "No one's going to eat it."

The new cake was a beauty. Toby packed it in a can. It made it easier to be taking something.

Other visitors were making their way purposefully up the neat driveway.

The main door, with its colored-glass segments, was hospitably open.

Inside, the smell of polish and disinfectant competed with each other. The floors were shiny. There were pictures on the walls. "On loan from the Municipal Library," ran the legend under them.

Toby attached himself to a young girl in starched apron and cap as she hurried across the hall.

"Mr. Penfold. Can I see Mr. Penfold, please?"

She stopped.

"Mr. Penfold, is it?" she asked, in a soft voice. "Well, of course. Just you wait a minute."

She came back almost immediately with a tall, crisp person.

"Matron, this is someone for Mr. Penfold."

The matron eyed Toby and crackled her cuffs. "I see," she said. "Children"—she repeated the word with distaste—"children are not usually encouraged to visit, *un*-supervised."

"Mr. Penfold—is *my* friend," said Toby.

The little girl whispered in Matron's ear.

"Ah," said the matron. "Ah, *that* one. I remember. Of course. Well, young man. You can visit him. But we don't want any more of that nasty publicity, do we? We're all the same here. All the same. Take him in."

"This way," whispered the girl.

She opened the swinging doors and pushed Toby through.

A sea of faces seemed to greet him, so that his eyes lost their focus. Many of the faces, turning sharply to the door, turned away as they saw they did not know him. Hardly daring to raise his eyes, Toby moved timidly along, searching.

He gave a little hum—make it casual, for heaven's sake. He was only making a visit.

He had gone past one armchair with its occupant when a voice said,

"Toby."

Toby turned, and gazed at what for a moment seemed a perfect stranger. Gone was the barrier of coats, gone now the hat and the gray hair and the straggling beard—all were shorn. Only the blue eyes were the same.

"Josh," said Toby. Curses, his voice sounded high with dismay. "Josh," he tried again. Better this time.

Josh put his hand up to touch the white portions of his face, where wind and sun had never reached before.

"Didn't recognize myself either," he said. "I feel half the size. What brings you here?"

"To see you, of course. I said I would," said Toby. "It was all I could do to stop Olly coming too."

"The little maid," Josh smiled. "I got her owl ready."

"I'll bring her next time. Here." Toby offered the cake. "It's made by Ma. Not me."

"Thank her very kindly," said Josh. He put it down with a faint, very faint sigh.

"You'd better give it in to the nurse, the one called Molly. We have to hand all our food in, and then it's shared out."

"Oh, pooh, what a shame," said Toby.

Toby took a look around. "They seem very old, most of them," he whispered.

"They are," whispered Josh. "Old in mind too. Can't make me out at all. Not in the mold, see. Different."

"Are you settled?" said Toby.

Josh's eyes twinkled.

"You might say, I'm a-settling," he said. "Mind you, gave them a bit of trouble at first. Had to calm me down and sweeten me up, so I could mix with them."

"Have you made any friends?" asked Toby, doubtfully.

He looked around. Pursed lips and sidelong glances surrounded them.

"Come and see my room," said Josh, changing the subject.

"Nice bed. Nice lamp. And I can see the woods from here."

Toby came and stood beside him.

"Do you miss it . . . very much . . . the woods, I mean?"

Josh looked out. He tapped his head.

"I carry it around in here," he said "All this . . ." He waved around at the room. "It's an experience, I can tell you. . . ."

Josh saw the other residents with sharp eyes, undulled with familiarity with the human face. One by one, he unraveled them for Toby. The bear, the shaggy man of the woods, became a clown. Toby laughed, until his eyes stung.

The bell rang. Sharp. Toby sobered quickly.

"I'll come again," he said.

Josh nodded. Beneath the starched shadow of the matron, he became small and acquiescent. He waved dutifully from the windows.

"Good-byee. Good-byee."

Toby sat up late that night, even after his light was out.

"Grow. Grow. Stretch," went his muscles, secretly, invisibly growing. Knobbly knees. Feet going on forever. He was growing. He was young—Toby stopped. He must be getting older to *know* that he was young.

The night air was cold. Starlight. Blood going slosh in his veins. Heart going—da, dum, da, dum—stopped. Toby waited. No—thank *you*, it had started again—da, dum.

Me. Me. Me, thought Toby. In other rooms, in other places, there were other people, who were "me" to themselves. Oh, Lord. It was all far too complicated. Especially late at night.

How come he hadn't thought of other people being "me" before? Growing. Growing. Stretch.

Toby shook his head. He thought of Josh. "Enjoy the day." He smiled.

"O.K., Josh," he said aloud.

The second visit came. Toby knew the way in. The antiseptic portals didn't quell him as before. Besides, he had Olly beside him. No nurse this time.

"He's in there," said Toby, and pushed open the doors of the lounge. It was just the same as before —but this time he really couldn't find Josh.

In case he had missed him, he peered carefully into each face. Olly tugged at his sleeve.

"Go on," she said. "*Find* him. You said he was in here."

"I'm looking, aren't I?" whispered Toby.

"Why are we whispering?"

"I don't know."

Olly giggled. "It's like the public library."

"Sh."

The matron was advancing upon them.

"Ah," she said. She eyed Olly, with her china stare. Her nose, faintly pink, twitched.

"Now I'm afraid you're going to be unlucky, young man."

Toby looked at her, uncomprehendingly.

"Mr. Penfold. Mr. Penfold has been foolish."

"Foolish," repeated Toby. It seemed such an odd word.

"He had a little cold and he went out. He got wet. He was advised—he was *told*—not to go. He is, I'm afraid, ill."

She glared at Toby, as if he were part of a conspiracy.

"Can't we see him, then?" said Olly.

"He's ill," repeated the matron, as if she were explaining to a very stupid person. "He is having *no* visitors."

She gave them a dismissive nod, and swept on.

"Well . . ." began Olly.

The little nurse came out and beckoned Toby.

"Here," she whispered. "You're looking for Mr. Penfold. I'll be in trouble, if I'm caught, but no matter. I'm sure he'd like a visitor. He talks of you, you know." Her face softened. "He's a grand man, like my grandfather. You come with me. But *shsh*."

Toby and Olly followed her down a corridor.

"It's the germs, you see," she rattled on. "Him being used to living in the fresh air, away from it all. He's got no resistance, see. Got a shocking cold—and wanted to breathe fresh air. Turned my back, and he was gone —not that I blame him—it's close in here sometimes.

Got much worse, you see. Here we are. Not for long, mind."

"Sick Bay," it said in red letters on the door.

Olly made gentle retching noises in her throat.

"How horrible," she said. "That's enough to stop anyone getting well."

The door opened. There was Josh, on a high, white bed. Pillows were piled behind him. His eyes were shut and his breath came in little rasps. High spots of color burned strangely like poppies on the white skin.

"Mr. Penfold," whispered Molly.

Josh's eyes opened. He saw Toby and Olly. The smile of greeting was stopped halfway by his coughing.

Molly crossed to an ominous black cylinder, which stood by his bed.

"Do you want some oxygen, Mr. Penfold?"

Josh shook his head.

Olly crossed over to him and took his hand.

"I'm sorry," she said. "You'll soon be better."

Toby stepped nearer, as Josh's gaze searched for him.

"Hi, Josh," he said softly.

Toby took his other hand and patted it. He quelled Olly with a look.

Josh pointed to his bedside table.

"It's that old can," said Molly. "He always takes it with him. You want it?"

88

Josh nodded. Another cough rose, leaving him gasping. With shaking hands, he undid it and took out the owl.

Olly took it gravely.

"It's the most beautiful carving I ever saw," she said. She gave him a quick kiss on his stubbly cheek, going pink as she did so, and eyeing Toby defiantly, in case he should tease her for it.

"Be better soon," said Josh. His eyes wandered and fixed on the patch of blue sky shining through the window.

"Almost spring," he said. "See it, Arthur."

"I see it," said Toby.

Josh lay back. His face looked very youthful, the blue of his eyes brilliant.

"Good boy . . ."

"It's time now—you must go—before the visitor's bell. Do you feel better for your having seen visitors, Mr. Penfold?"

Josh nodded. He did look better—brighter and more alert. He raised a hand and half saluted them as they went through the door.

Molly spirited them along the mercifully empty corridors and out into the sunshine.

Toby and Olly blinked. The brightness was stunning. They walked along in silence for a while.

"He's ill," said Olly.

"Clever you," said Toby.

"All the things he told you. Are they all in your essay?"

"Most," said Toby. "They don't look so good written. It's the way he says it."

Olly looked at Toby.

"He likes you," she said. "A lot."

Toby went red. "Even after—?"

"After what?"

"Well, you know, it was my fault he was ever found. He wouldn't be where he is if it hadn't been for me."

Olly stood still. Stock still.

"For heaven's sake. Don't stand there in the middle of a street crossing."

Toby dragged Olly across. She was chewing her hair.

"Do you realize," she said, "that *everything, everything* we do is important? Have you ever thought of that? We can't even breathe without someone breathing out somewhere. It's a chain. Most times we don't see what happens. But it happens just the same. What I do will change something for someone. Oh, Toby, I'm scared to breathe again."

"Then you'll be pretty dead," said Toby.

Olly let out the breath she had so dramatically held.

"It is true, isn't it," she said.

"It's true," said Toby. "But you can't think about it all the time or you'd go mad."

Olly looked at him, suddenly older than ten years, woman older.

"Don't be miserable," she said. "It'll be all right."

"Of course it will."

"And, Toby."

"Yes."

"I like you—a lot—too."

"Well . . ." Toby was embarrassed. "Thank you, Miss Olly. You're not so bad yourself. . . ."

Chapter Ten

"Just a moment."

This time it was the matron who stopped him as soon as he stepped in the door, carrying flowers—early spring flowers.

She cleared her throat and shot her cuffs up and down.

"I'm afraid," she said, "you can't go in. Mr. Penfold is no longer . . . with us."

Toby looked at her. "No longer with you," he repeated.

"I'm very sorry," said the matron.

"But . . . where's he gone?"

Matron was taken aback. "My dear child. I'm trying . . . trying to tell you. You must have known he was a very sick man."

Thick cotton was fastened around Toby's head. Sound got caught up in it. Voices came at the end of a long tunnel.

"He died last night."

Died. Died. Died. The words came and went, now near, now far.

The matron nodded uneasily. She moved off. Toby turned. A cool hand took him.

"Come along, love." It was the nurse.

Toby stared at her. His eyes were black in his face.

"I'm ever so sorry. He was a lovely man. He thought a lot of you."

"I killed him."

"No, you never."

"Yes, I did." Toby was cold. "I sent him here, and he died."

"Oh, he had a bad chest. It would have caught up with him soon. He was an ill man, truly he was. He wouldn't have had very long."

Toby shook off her comforting arm.

"It was coming here—in with all the germs, you said. That did it. It was me. My fault."

Eyes looked at him helplessly. "Here, he wanted to give you this."

Toby thrust the can away.

The nurse's color rose.

"That's a fine way to carry on. Just you take it, my lad. He said it was for you."

Toby stood. She thrust the can into his hands and closed his stiff fingers around it.

"You go on home," she said gently.

Through the skin of his fingers, Toby could feel the can, and inside, the penknife and the carvings. Cold. Cold.

"You deaf and blind, sonny?"

A car screeched to a halt as he stepped blindly off the curb.

The enormity of what had happened swelled in Toby's mind. People's faces and mouths moved, eyes and teeth glinted. Under water. Waving images. A dead bird, lying squashed in the gutter, made sickness rise in him.

He walked more quickly. One. Two. Automation. One. Two. Robot Man. Faster. Into the woods. Trees whipping, closing on him. Silence pursuing him.

Carefully, carefully in the clearing, he put down the can. The sun shone. Two robins flew down.

"He's dead," said Toby aloud.

The birds hopped hopefully.

Toby ran at them.

"Stupid! Stupid! He's dead, I tell you. Didn't you *hear*? He's *never* coming back anymore."

The birds panicked away. Toby ran around the thicket, tearing, slashing, pulling down, trampling underfoot.

His breath came in great gasps. The trees waited.

"There! There! There! Gone! Gone!"

At last, shuddering, he stopped. The clearing filled up with sun and silence.

"Enjoy the day."

Toby dropped down on the mossy turf and wept. He cried for his mother, dead so long ago. He cried for himself and his father, being left. He cried for Ma and Olly, because he had pushed them away. He cried for Josh, who had been big and brave under his many coats—who had known how to live.

He cried for the boy, at the beginning of the year, who would never be the same again. . . . He cried until the tears stiffened on his cheeks and he felt light and clean and washed, as if he were reborn.

Under his eyes, minute insects struggled to heave a twig over white-flowered moss, no larger than a pin's head. Almost a sleepiness overtook him.

Lie there forever.

A shadow fell.

Toby raised his head.

Ma stood there.

"They phoned," she said. "I knew you'd be here."

Toby got up slowly. He picked up the can. Ma stood there. Mountain. Sure, solid mountain. Rock. She put a comfortable arm around him.

Toby leaned his aching head against her shoulder.

Silently they both looked at the clearing. Pale images seemed to flicker by and disappear.

Toby shook himself. He clasped the can firmly under his arm.

"Let's go home," he said.